MAX FLASH
MISSION 4
GRAVE DANGER

For all staff and pupils at:
Mulberry Primary School
Osidge Primary School
Brookland Junior School
And thanks to Sonny Turner, the winner of the Max Flash Gadget
Competition with his Laser Stunner

Text copyright © Jonny Zucker, 2008
Illustrations copyright © Ned Woodman, 2008

"Mission 4: Grave Danger" was originally published in English in 2008. This edition is
published by an arrangement with STRIPES PUBLISHING, an imprint of Magi Publications.

Copyright © 2013 by Darby Creek

Darby Creek
A division of Lerner Publishing Group, Inc.
241 First Avenue North
Minneapolis, MN 55401 U.S.A.

Website address: www.lernerbooks.com

Library of Congress Cataloging-in-Publication Data

Zucker, Jonny.
Grave danger / by Jonny Zucker ; illustrated by Ned Woodman.
pages   cm. — (Max Flash ; mission 4)
Originally published in the United Kingdom by Stripes Publishing, 2008.
Summary: "Max Flash, explosive escapologist and master magician, is back for his fourth
death-defying mission. The Department for Extraordinary Activity tells Max that the *Sorceror's
Venom*, an ancient Egyptian papyrus, has been stolen. Legend has it that the papyrus holds
the power to raise the dead, so Max must prepare himself for a gruesome battle."— Provided
by publisher.
ISBN 978–1–4677–1210–1 (lib. bdg. : alk. paper)
ISBN 978–1–4677–2054–0 (eBook)
[1. Egypt—Antiquities—Fiction. 2. Dead—Fiction. 3. Adventure and adventurers—Fiction.]
I. Woodman, Ned, 1978– illustrator. II. Title.
PZ7.Z77925Gr 2013
[Fic]—dc23   2012049022

Manufactured in the United States of America
1 – BP – 7/15/13

MISSION 4
GRAVE DANGER

Jonny Zucker

Illustrated by
Ned Woodman

CHAPTER 1

Max Flash kept his body low. He crept down the dark corridor. His right hand gripped a black Laser Bolt gun. He looked around for signs of attackers. Up ahead of him, a tiny circle of light appeared.

The Escape Dimension! I knew I was on the right track!

But as Max took another step, an archway to his left flew up. One of the Killer Zombies appeared. Its twisted body gave off a fuzzy silver glow. The Zombie put a Death Blower to its slimy lips. The Zombie blew into the small brown pipe.

A steel bubble grew at the end of the Death Blower. It crashed towards Max, growing larger by the second. Max raised the Laser Bolt gun. He fired.

His aim was perfect.

Max ducked. He covered his head. The bubble exploded into a million pieces.

Max ran on. He headed toward the light. Within ten meters, his path was blocked. Three more Zombies appeared. Max didn't stop. Before they could raise their Blowers, Max quickly fired three laser bolts. The Zombies collapsed to the ground. One by one, they melted into orangey yellow puddles.

Gross!

Max leaped over these steaming pools. He sprinted away. A large, neon-blue sign suddenly flashed right in front of his face.

EXERCISE INTERRUPTED! it said in huge letters.

Max cursed.

Things were just getting interesting!

He pulled off his Virtual Battle Helmet. He squinted at the bright lights of the communications center located in his basement.

Max watched as Zavonne's face appeared on the large plasma screen. She looked as usual. Her hair was pulled tightly back off her face. She fixed Max with her trademark frosty stare.

"Hey, Zavonne," said Max.

"Hello, Max," she said briskly. "I'm sorry to interrupt your zombie-fighting practice. But something has come up that requires immediate attention."

CHAPTER 2

A while back, Zavonne had recruited Max
as a DFEA operative. The Department for
Extraordinary Activity specialized in unusual
happenings. It investigated things that the
official authorities knew nothing about. If it
involved invisible beasts crawling through
under-city pipes or slipping back into the great
battles of history, it was a case for the DFEA.

Max had been recruited partly because
his parents were operatives. Montgomery
and Carly Flash were highly experienced

stage magicians. They had a flair for creating illusions. This made them perfect DFEA recruits.

Max's parents had done two missions for Zavonne. Zavonne had recently turned to Max. Max had picked up all sorts of tricks and illusions watching his parents perform. But Max also had another skill his parents didn't. He had an incredibly flexible body. He could squeeze into, or out of, the tiniest spaces.

Zavonne had decided Max was perfect for the DFEA. He'd been on three incredible missions so far. They had taken him into virtual reality, to distant galaxies, and deep below the sea.

Max stared up at Zavonne's face on the screen. One thought came into his head.

What has Zavonne got in mind this time?

As usual, she wasted no time.

"Two weeks ago there was a fierce sandstorm two miles east of the Denubi Pyramid in Egypt. After the storm, some locals found several large stones that had been uncovered by the winds. These stones were part of a large, ancient building."

Max listened. Zavonne was an ice queen. But her missions always brought unexpected adventures and lots of danger!

"The area was immediately sealed off," she continued. "One of the world's top archaeologists, Professor Edmund Blythe, was called to the scene. After Blythe looked at the find, he declared that the building was the legendary Palace of Golden Kings—home to the boy pharaoh Gazellion."

Max knew a bit about ancient Egypt. He'd actually listened in school when they were studying it. Especially the part about the gory process of mummification.

Disgusting, yet fascinating!

"Gazellion was only your age when he was killed defending his palace. His attacker was a man named Tulamen," said Zavonne. "After Gazellion's death, Tulamen became pharaoh."

Where is she heading with this one?

"As was the custom, Gazellion should have been buried with all of his gold and jewels inside the Denubi Pyramid."

"*Should* have?" asked Max.

Zavonne nodded. "The pyramid was first excavated seventy years ago. A burial chamber was found. But there was no sign of any gold or jewels. Three mummies were found in sarcophagi. But none of them was the mummy of Gazellion. All three belonged to his servants."

"But how did they know that one of them wasn't Gazellion?"

"In two of the sarcophagi were sets of basic serving utensils. In the third the excavators found a piece of papyrus swearing allegiance to Gazellion. It was clear that they all came from the serving class."

"OK," said Max, scratching his head. "Then where was Gazellion's mummy buried?"

"No one knows," said Zavonne. "Exhaustive searches were made. But no sign of his burial chamber or his mummy were ever found. The whole place was sealed to prevent robbers from entering the tomb."

"Weird," mused Max.

"No," said Zavonne darkly. "That's not the weird part. That's only the background."

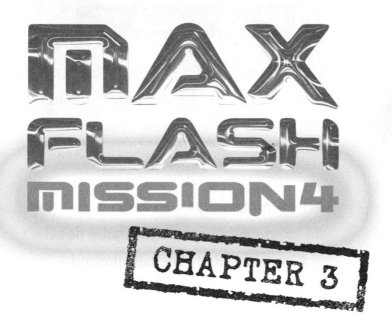

CHAPTER 3

"Two days ago," said Zavonne, "Professor Blythe's team found a fascinating piece of papyrus in the palace."

A slot on the wall next to Max bleeped. Out slid a sheet of paper. It was a copy of the papyrus. It was covered with tiny black-and-gold hieroglyphs. It pictured mythical beasts. These beasts included a two-headed crocodile and a hippo wearing a collar of razor-sharp blades. The border was decorated with terrifying green and silver snakes.

"What does it say?" asked Max.

"We don't know," replied Zavonne. "Neither do Professor Blythe and his team. None of them has ever seen hieroglyphs like these. I've sent this out to several DFEA Egyptologists. But so far, no one has been able to translate it. However, we think we have identified the papyrus."

"What do you think it is?" asked Max.

"We think it might be the *Sorcerer's Venom*."

Cool name!

"According to legend, this papyrus has dark and dangerous powers. Including the power to bring the dead back to life. It's said that it was passed down from pharaoh to pharaoh. No one knows who created the *Sorcerer's Venom*. Most archaeologists, including Professor Blythe, don't believe it exists. To Blythe, it is a fascinating historical document. But it has no special powers."

"Where is it now?"

Zavonne looked at Max with her crystal-clear eyes. "Last night, a van left the dig site with the papyrus. Professor Blythe ordered for it to be moved to a museum in Cairo. There, a number of specialists would get a chance to study it."

Max nodded.

"But the van never got there. It was discovered early this morning. It was parked fifty meters from the Denubi Pyramid. It was completely burned out. The driver was in severe shock. He was shivering and sputtering. He said something about being attacked by the Serpents of Death. There was no sign of the papyrus."

Max looked down at the paper in his hand. He stared at the evil-looking snakes on its border.

"The Egyptian police say the papyrus must have been stolen by art thieves," stated Zavonne. "But I fear that darker forces are at work. If this papyrus is the *Sorcerer's Venom* and it gets into the wrong hands, who knows what might happen?"

Max swallowed nervously.

"Two of my operatives are leaving later today for the dig site," said Zavonne. "They are Mike Cullen and Sarah Dodd. Both of them are first-class Egyptologists. They'll be extremely useful to Professor Blythe. The professor is very strict about those who work

with him on digs. He insists that his whole
team be dedicated to the dig 24/7. He does
not permit anyone to leave the site. As a
result, Cullen and Dodd's movements will be
restricted. And that's where you come in."

"Er . . . I know a bit about ancient Egypt,"
said Max. "But I'm not what you'd call a fully
loaded Egyptologist."

Zavonne ignored this and continued. "Your
cover story is that Cullen and Dodd are your
parents. Their childcare arrangements fell
through at the last minute. They had no
choice but to bring you along on the dig."

"And this Professor guy is cool about that?"
asked Max.

Zavonne frowned. "Professor Blythe did not
warm to the idea. In fact, he put up quite a
fight. But we pulled some strings with the
people who funded his dig. He had no choice
in the matter."

Great! Zavonne's sending me out to a dig

site where the main man will hate my guts!

Zavonne looked at Max with her steely eyes. "As well as doing their work on the site, Cullen and Dodd will be there to provide round-the-clock backup for you," she explained. "You won't be a member of Professor Blythe's team. So you will be in a unique position. You'll be able to slip in and out of the dig site to investigate the theft. In addition, your contortion and escapology skills will come in handy. Sites like this often have tiny openings an adult could never get into."

Max thought this over. On his first three missions he'd worked alone. Having fellow operatives on board could be excellent. But if they were as cold as Zavonne, it could be deathly.

"Your mission is to find the *Sorcerer's Venom* and retrieve it," said Zavonne. "Like I said, we think it has fallen into the wrong hands. We are very concerned that whoever

has it wants to use its immense powers in the name of evil."

"And if I don't get it back?" asked Max.

"That is not an option, Max," replied Zavonne. "You have one task. Find the papyrus and bring it back to me."

MAX FLASH MISSION4

CHAPTER 4

Zavonne eyed Max seriously. "This is a dangerous mission, Max. There are powers at work we know nothing about. If the papyrus is as deadly and magical as we think, you must proceed with extreme caution. Your life will be in constant danger. We have gadgets that were made especially for the dangers of this mission."

Max felt a surge of excitement. *Gadget time! Bring them on!*

A red drawer in the wall slid open.

"Take out the top item," said Zavonne.

Max picked up what looked like a football trading card. It had a picture of a player throwing a ball. "That is a Rock-Solid Scanner," Zavonne explained. "If you press the card flat against any surface—even rock—it will show you any object up to two meters behind that surface. It will work for five minutes."

Max turned the trading card over.

Looking through walls? Excellent!

"The second item is a Frisbee Hover-Board."

Max pulled out a neon-green Frisbee. "Throw this Frisbee into the air. It will return to you in the form of a hover-board. You can fly on this board for one minute at sixty miles per hour."

Max felt the smooth surface of the Frisbee.

Flying at sixty miles per hour. Cool!

"The last gadget is called a Laser Stunner," said Zavonne.

Max held up a chunky bracelet. It had blue and gold beads on it.

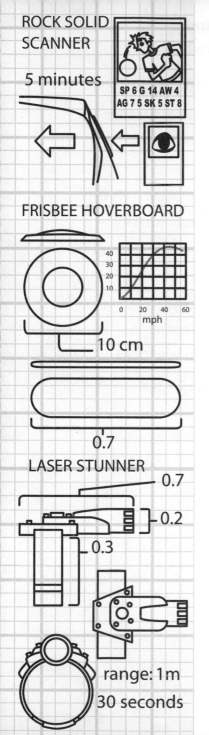

ROCK SOLID SCANNER

5 minutes

SP 6 G 14 AW 4
AG 7 5 SK 5 ST 8

FRISBEE HOVERBOARD

40
30
20
10

0   20   40   60
mph

10 cm

0.7

LASER STUNNER

0.7

0.2

0.3

range: 1 m

30 seconds

"When you press that small button, the bracelet will fire a laser. It will stun any attacker and give you thirty seconds to escape."

Max slipped on the bracelet. It fit perfectly.

This could come in handy, Max thought.

"Remember," Zavonne cautioned, "these gadgets should only be used to escape from immediate danger. They are not toys."

"Yes, Zavonne," sighed Max.

How many times do I have to listen to this speech?

"Your plane leaves in two hours. Your father will

drive you to the airport. Cullen and Dodd will be waiting there. The three of you will catch a flight to Cairo, Egypt. A car will meet you and take you to the dig site."

Max took in all of these details.

"And Max," said Zavonne, "this is not a vacation. I need you to find that papyrus—and fast."

But before Max could reply, the image of Zavonne had disappeared from the screen.

MAX FLASH MISSION4

CHAPTER 5

Max's dad drove him to the airport. He seemed worried about the mission.

"It sounds dangerous, Max," he said.

"But I've got great gadgets. And Cullen and Dodd are my backup," Max pointed out.

"True," replied his dad. "But just take extra care. Your mom and I want you to come home alive. Not in some coffin."

Max swallowed nervously.

What kind of deathly challenges will I be facing?

Cullen and Dodd were waiting in the airport. Dad hugged Max good-bye. He wished all three of them luck. They had an hour before their plane boarded. They had time to grab a drink.

Sarah Dodd was a serious woman. She had hazel eyes and frizzy brown hair. She looked like the kind of person who didn't laugh much.

She and Zavonne probably get on great!

Mike Cullen was more relaxed. He had short brown hair and a dimple in his chin. Like Dodd, he was very focused on the mission. But

it seemed to Max that he probably had a life outside of his work for the DFEA.

"We'll use our first names," explained Cullen. "But our last name will be Taylor."

Max Taylor. It sounded OK.

Dodd pulled out a map of the dig site. "Our living quarters are over there." She pointed. "And the main focus of the dig is here."

Max studied the map. It was weird to think they'd be in Egypt in a few hours. And they'd be looking for an ancient piece of papyrus.

"As you know, Professor Blythe is very strict," said Cullen. "He likes to be in control. So Dodd and I will pretty much be at his beck and call."

"But we'll support you in whatever way we can," added Dodd. She almost smiled.

Maybe she's not quite as robotic as Zavonne!

"Obviously, anything we do must be top secret," said Cullen. "As far as the professor

is concerned, the missing papyrus is just a document of academic interest. It is not a nest of evil spirits and curses. We have to keep him completely in the dark about what we're doing. If he suspects for one minute that we have another agenda, he'll kick us out without hesitation."

"Understood," said Max.

CHAPTER 6

The flight to Cairo was nearly empty. Max and his "parents" had plenty of room to stretch out. Max listened to music on his EX4 player for a while. Then he fell asleep. He woke up when the plane landed. It was early evening.

Max stepped onto the steps leading out of the plane. The heat hit him like a body blow. The sun was burning golden-orange.

Inside the terminal, the three DFEA operatives made their way through passport control. They headed outside. A man was

waiting beside a black jeep. He held a piece of cardboard with the words, "TAYLOR FAMILY."

He shoved their bags in the back. They wound through busy streets for an hour. Then they left the city behind. There didn't seem to be any speed limit out on the desert roads. The driver floored the gas pedal.

It was now eight o'clock. Darkness was falling. Cullen was sitting up front with the driver. Max was in the back with Dodd. Up ahead he could see a faint ring of lights. Beyond them rose the huge, imposing shape of the Denubi Pyramid.

A few minutes later, the dig site was in view. Max was amazed. It was a massive rectangular area the size of four football fields. A high metal fence surrounded the whole place. No one on the outside could look in.

"Security is necessary," the driver told them. "The pieces they find on the dig are priceless. Looters are known to try their luck."

Max thought about the stolen papyrus. *Is it*

the Sorcerer's Venom? *How hard will it be to get back?*

The jeep pulled up beside a large archway. Two Egyptian soldiers with machine guns stood on either side. The driver handed one of them some papers.

The soldier shone his flashlight on the papers. He then stepped into a small sentry box. He came out a few seconds later holding three laminated passes on lengths of elastic. He handed these to the driver.

"You must wear these at all times," the driver said. "Security is very tight."

The soldier waved them on. The jeep eased forward. They drove down a wide track and pulled into a parking lot. Max could see the dig site up ahead.

The driver pointed at an area about twenty meters to the right. There were a large group of tents.

"Accommodation," he explained. To the left were six large open-air tents. "Canteen,

showers, and research centers," he added. He got out of the jeep. Max, Cullen, and Dodd followed. The driver went to the back of the jeep to get the bags. They thanked him and then walked over to their sleeping quarters.

Cullen and Dodd were given a two-person tent. Max was delighted when he was given a two-person tent of his own.

Excellent—a double tent to myself! Plenty of room to spread out.

He went inside, put down his backpack, and took out his sleeping bag. He tied open the front flap of the tent. He sat down in the doorway and looked out across the site.

A few minutes later, Cullen and Dodd came out of their tent.

"Come on, Max," said Cullen. "Let's get some supper."

"How's your accommodation?" asked Dodd as they headed toward the canteen.

"Good," replied Max. "But I'm disappointed there's no swimming pool!"

"Yeah," said Cullen. "I brought my swimsuit. But somehow I don't think I'll get to use it."

Max laughed. Dodd kind of smiled.

The canteen was in one of the huge tents they'd seen when they first came. As they approached, they could hear the buzz of conversation.

The canteen was a hub of activity and noise. Several long serving tables stood at the far end. Chefs served food from large metal vats. The rest of the tent was filled with long tables and benches. People there were wearing coveralls and khaki uniforms.

"There's a lot of people here," observed Max. They wove their way through the tables.

"It's huge," agreed Cullen. "But the Palace of Golden Kings is one of the best finds in the history of archaeology. They need a massive team. The stuff they're finding isn't just

priceless. It also tells us a great deal about how the ancient Egyptians lived."

They reached the serving tables. They were being asked what they'd like to eat when a sandy-haired man with thin eyebrows and blue eyes came over. He had a serious expression on his face.

"That's Professor Blythe," whispered Dodd.

The professor stopped in front of them. "Taylor and Taylor, I presume," he said. He shook hands with Cullen and Dodd.

Max reached out to shake his hand, too. But the professor pulled his hand away. He stared at Max with a withering look.

"I have never had a child on a dig before," said the professor, lowering his voice. "And I never intend to have one again."

Great to meet you, too!

"I'm sure you've heard the phrase, 'out of sight, out of mind'," said the professor. "That description will apply to you. I don't want you anywhere near the excavations. It is not a place for a child. Do you understand?"

"Yes," replied Max, trying not to get too angry.

"Right, then," said the professor. He turned back to Cullen and Dodd. "I'll see you both in Examination Tent Two in ten minutes. There's a piece of a jug I'd like you to look at."

"We'll be there," said Dodd.

The professor turned and bustled away.

"He seemed really pleased to meet me, didn't he?" groaned Max.

"Don't worry about him," smiled Cullen. "He's just like the things he finds on his digs. A relic!"

CHAPTER 7

To Max's surprise, the food wasn't that bad. He had some pita bread, salad, and a slice of apple cake. During the meal, he talked with Cullen and Dodd about their mission.

They agreed that Max would visit the site of the burned-out van tonight. It might give them some clues about who the thieves were.

"Don't spend too long there," warned Dodd. "Have a quick look about. Then come back. We'll meet up later at the tents."

Max finished his supper. He said good-bye

to his "parents" and walked off. He double-checked that his gadgets were tucked safely inside his backpack. He headed up the path.

The guards had been told by Cullen and Dodd that Max was working on a school project about life in the desert. He should be able to come and go as he pleased. Max approached the two guards at the main entrance. They nodded and waved him through.

In the distance he could see the outline of the Denubi Pyramid. He'd figured that he'd be able to get there in about a half hour. The air was cooler. His calculations were spot on. In twenty-seven minutes he was standing one hundred meters from the base of the pyramid.

Fifty meters away sat the burned-out Range Rover. It looked twisted and broken. Max walked over. He shone his flashlight across it. The material on the seats was charred and flaking.

But who attacked the vehicle? And why was
the driver in such a state of shock?

Max walked past the Range Rover. He
headed towards the pyramid. But he'd only
gone five paces when he was attacked.

At first, he figured the lines on the ground

were just shadows. But then his flashlight picked out a series of slithery, twisting shapes. The creatures gave off a green-and-silver glow.

Snakes!

He leaped backwards in horror and started to run.

CHAPTER 8

The snakes were incredibly speedy. As Max
fled, he could feel them lashing out at him.
They tried to wrap themselves around his
ankles.

The Serpents of Death! The jeep driver
hadn't been seeing things. He must have been
attacked by this army of vipers! They were the
papyrus thieves!

Max kicked as hard as he could. But the
snakes kept striking at him. There were
hundreds of them! Max ran. He reached into

his backpack and pulled out the Frisbee.

Two snakes were curling round each shin.
He was being dragged backward. If he didn't
move fast, the snakes would have him on the
ground. In desperation, he threw the Frisbee
into the air.

It made a fizzing sound. It crashed to the
ground in the shape of a hover-board. It flew
to Max.

Thank you, Zavonne!

It took every ounce of strength. Max twisted
and wriggled away. He kicked at the attacking
snakes. He jumped onto the board. As soon as
his feet made contact, he catapulted into the air.

Yessssssss!

The board sped off. Max hurtled towards
the pyramid. In the light of the full moon, he
saw the snakes right below him. Their forked
tongues were spitting out in frenzy.

*I need to lose these slithering poison
shooters!*

Max flew alongside the pyramid. He searched its stone surface for an opening. The snakes were speeding up the pyramid's side. They waited for Max to fall into their path. For the first few seconds, Max only saw solid rock. But then something near the top caught his eye. It was a small circle of black. There was an opening about twenty meters away. He flew straight toward it. The snakes hissed with fury below him.

He was ten meters away when the board suddenly made a low humming sound. It started losing speed.

No! The sixty seconds must be up! I'm snake feed!

Max fell through the air toward the snakes. The snakes were speeding up the side of the pyramid. He crashed against the pyramid. He began to slide down. He threw out his hand for any possible handhold. The snakes were nearly upon him. They looked like a huge, moving oil slick. Their slimy bodies twisted as they gained on their prey.

Just as he was about to fall into their clutches, Max's hand brushed against a small fragment of rock. It was his only chance. He grabbed it.

The snakes were now centimeters away. Max pulled as hard as he could on the handhold. He began to climb back up the pyramid.

Up and up the crumbling side of the pyramid he went. He was using both feet and both hands. But he still kept slipping.

Where is that opening?

His hands were red by now. But he knew he had to keep going.

He looked around for a

45

second. Big mistake. The snakes were faster than he was. It would only be a matter of time before they reached him.

But then his hand fell forward. He realized he had found the opening he'd seen moments before. Max swung around and squeezed his body through the hole.

He dropped about three meters before hitting the ground. He got to his feet. He quickly took off his backpack. He threw it up so it wedged into the opening. He could still hear the hiss of the snakes.

Max breathed a huge sigh of relief. *That was close!* He wiped a line of sweat from his forehead. He looked around.

He'd fallen into a narrow passageway. Behind him it went up and to the left. In front of him it went down and to the right.

Max pulled out his flashlight. He started heading down.

He'd barely gone ten paces when he heard a

noise behind him. He spun around. He saw two figures on the path behind him.

He froze in terror.

The figures were wrapped in tight, white bandages. They both had identical amulets around their necks. The amulets were shaped like scarab beetles. One had a blue amulet. The other's was green. Max could see their dark grey eyes staring out at him through slits in the face area. Their thin, unsmiling lips framed rows of hideously decayed and jagged teeth.

Euuurghhh! Mummies brought back from the dead!

CHAPTER 9

Max shone his flashlight in the mummies' faces. He was trying to blind them for a few seconds so he could escape. He started down the passage. One of the mummies called after him.

"If you turn down that cursed orb of light and state who you are, we will not attack you!"

Max slowed his pace. *Should I trust a mummy from ancient Egypt? But what choice do I have? I don't know where this passageway goes. And who knows if there are more of these creatures down there?*

Max came to a stop. He turned around and shone his flashlight at the floor.

OK. Time for a chat. But if those mummies try to pull a fast one, I'm heading back down that passage—wherever it leads.

"State who you are!" commanded the mummy with the green amulet.

"I . . . I . . . I'm Max." He walked toward them.

There's clearly some kind of magic at work. Something brought these mummies back from the dead. Maybe they know something about the Sorcerer's Venom . . .

"Declare the name of that mystical beam of light," said the one with the blue amulet.

"It's called a flashlight," Max answered.

He turned it off, and the passageway fell into half-darkness.

"Max and flashlight!" said the one with the blue amulet. It leaned forward so that its face was almost touching Max's. "I've never heard such names."

Max took a couple of steps back.

This guy's breath could kill a whole army!

"I'm out here with my parents," Max explained. "We're trying to find a special piece of papyrus called the *Sorcerer's Venom*. Do you know anything about it?" he asked. He sounded braver than he felt.

The mummies exchanged a quick glance. They stepped back and held a quick, whispered conversation.

"You haven't told me your names," said Max.

They fell silent. They advanced toward him again. But Max stood his ground.

"I am Idris," said the one with the blue amulet.

"And I am Sirus," said the other. "Your flashlight will interest the Mystical One. Return here tomorrow morning. Bring it with you."

"And you'll tell me about the papyrus?" asked Max hopefully.

"Just come back here," said Idris.

"What about those extra-friendly serpents out there?" asked Max. "Won't they attack me when I leave?"

"They will not bother you," said Sirus. "They only attack those who approach the pyramid. You are leaving. They won't touch you."

"Well what about when I come back?" pointed out Max. "They'll eat me for breakfast."

"The Mystical One will call them off," said Idris. "Now begone."

Max wanted to ask them more about the *Sorcerer's Venom*. But it was clear that the conversation was over.

"We will expect you tomorrow," Sirus added. The pair disappeared down the passage.

Max thought about following them. But he was keen to get back and report his run-in to Cullen and Dodd. So instead he headed back up the passage. He shone his flashlight over the wall. There were some places where

the stone had crumbled away. He could use those as footholds. He listened. There were no snakes. He clambered up and slipped on his backpack. He squeezed himself through the opening.

He looked left and right to check for his slithering foes.

But the coast was clear—just as the mummies had promised.

This didn't stop Max constantly checking behind him as he scrambled down the side of the pyramid; nor did it stop him running all the way back to the site.

CHAPTER 10

Cullen and Dodd were waiting for Max. They were seated around a small, square table. They motioned for him to sit down. Cullen brewed up some cocoa on a gas stove.

"What did you find?" asked Dodd.

"Quite a lot, actually!" said Max. He was relieved to be back. He told them of his narrow escape from the snakes. He recounted his meeting with the mummies. And he ended with his run back to the dig site.

With each sentence, Cullen and Dodd's eyes

grew larger. And their faces turned whiter.

"Mummies coming back from the dead," whispered Cullen. "This is bad news."

Max pulled a piece of paper out of his pocket. It was the copy of the papyrus that Zavonne had given him. He placed it on the table in front of Cullen and Dodd. "Those snakes looked exactly like the ones on the papyrus," he said. "That must be why the Range Rover driver went on about the Serpents of Death. It looks like those were the snakes that attacked him, too. Perhaps they stole the *Sorcerer's Venom*."

"And from what the mummies told you," wondered Dodd, "it's the Mystical One that's controlling the snakes. He must have the papyrus now."

"There's one thing I don't understand," said Cullen. "If this Mystical One already has the *Sorcerer's Venom*, why hasn't he used it yet? Surely he's brought those mummies back to life. And unleashed the snakes. But that seems to be it . . . What's he waiting for?"

"Good point," said Dodd.

The three of them were lost in thought for a few moments.

"Well, at least I know what my job is tomorrow," said Max. "I'll go to the pyramid. I'll find the papyrus. And I'll steal it back before the Mystical One or anyone else can unleash its evil powers."

Dodd bit her lip. "I don't think it will be that easy," she said. "And I'm not sure you should go back there alone. I don't like the sound of those mummies. What if they lied to you? What if this Mystical One doesn't call off the snakes?"

Cullen took a deep breath and blew out his cheeks. "It's a risk we're going to have to take," he said. "Professor Blythe will know if the two of us leave the site. It could jeopardize the whole mission."

"You're right," agreed Dodd. "But I still don't like it."

She is so not like Zavonne. She has emotions!

"I'll be fine," Max said with a smile. But inside he felt scared. There was something about those mummies that freaked him out!

Cullen stood up. "Well, we all need a good night's sleep," he advised. "Tomorrow could be a very long day."

Max nodded. Suddenly he realized he was exhausted. Fighting off a giant army of snakes and meeting two mummies wasn't the most relaxing way to spend an evening.

CHAPTER 11

Max woke early. He climbed out of his tent. He stretched his aching limbs. His escape from the snakes last night had taken its toll. His sleeping bag was well padded. But the sand beneath the tent wasn't as comfy as his bed at home. After washing his face and brushing his teeth, he felt a lot better.

He grabbed breakfast in the canteen with Cullen and Dodd. They were just finishing when Professor Blythe stopped to tell them about some rare chair he'd found. The

professor seemed not to notice Max at all.
So he murmured good-bye to his "parents."
He picked up his backpack from the tent and
slipped out.

It had been warm last night. But in the full
glare of the morning sun, it was baking. In
fact, it was so hot that Max thought he might
melt. As he walked, he thought about the
Sorcerer's Venom.

Would it be somewhere obvious in the
pyramid? Or would it be fiendishly difficult to
find? And who was this Mystical One?

He approached the burned-out vehicle. His
eyes darted all around. He was tense and
alert in case the snakes struck again. But all
was quiet. There was no sign of them. He was
drenched in sweat by the time he scrambled
up the side of the pyramid. It was a relief to
slip through the opening into the cool, dark
interior.

There was no sign of Idris or Sirus. As he

dropped down into the passageway, he could hear their voices in the distance. He flicked on his flashlight and followed the downward passage. It bent to the right, then to the left, then to the right again.

After several more turns, he saw an opening up ahead. A light shone out. He switched off his flashlight and walked on. The voices grew louder. They were joined by a third, much deeper voice.

That must be the Mystical One!

It was hard to hear what they were saying. But he did hear the word "rejoin." Just before he got to the end of the passage, Max heard Sirus say something about the Mystical One's powers being "diminished."

What does he mean?

The end of the passage opened into a chamber with three sarcophagi to the left. It was twice the size of his bedroom. But the ceiling was much lower.

The servants' burial chamber.

He peered in.

Idris and Sirus were standing with a third mummy. It was a head taller than the other two. It had no amulet around its neck.

Max looked around the chamber. He hoped to spot the *Sorcerer's Venom*. But it was nowhere to be seen.

He took a step forward.

"That's him!" declared Sirus, spotting Max.

The Mystical One stared across the chamber. He strode toward Max. Idris and Sirus followed at his side.

"Are you the one that possesses the magic orb?" he demanded.

Max nodded cautiously.

"I demand that you show it to me!"

Didn't they teach them any manners in ancient Egypt?

"And you are . . . ?" asked Max.

"I am Kalunga. The Mystical One. Sorcerer to

the mighty Pharaoh Gazellion!"

Max thought about what Zavonne had told him about Gazellion not being buried inside the pyramid.

"Go on, then!" snapped Kalunga impatiently. "Proceed!"

Max hesitated. "I will demonstrate it. But first I want to know if you have the *Sorcerer's Venom*."

Nothing like coming straight out with a question!

Kalunga stared at Max with contempt. "I only have what is rightfully mine!" snapped the Mystical One. "My snakes took care of that! Now begin the demonstration."

So he does have it! If it's so secretive and deadly, why did he admit that so easily?

"Er, where are you keeping it?" Max asked.

"ENOUGH QUESTIONS!" barked Kalunga. "I need to see the orb! If you fail to show it to me, the punishment will be BEYOND SEVERE!"

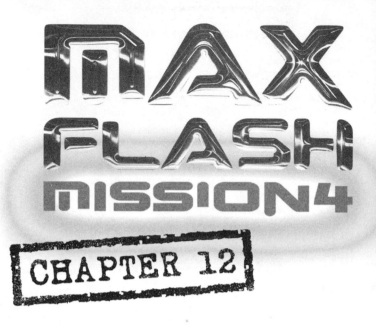

MAX FLASH
MISSION4

Max took a deep breath. He switched on the flashlight and swung its beam around the chamber. He held the beam on the ceiling for a few seconds. Then he switched it off.

"Fascinating," murmured Kalunga. He stared at the flashlight with interest.

"You can hold it," offered Max.

Kalunga took the flashlight. He turned it over in his hands.

"I order you to bring me ten thousand of these immediately!" declared Kalunga. "Each

member of my army should have one of its own."

Max looked up and down the passage. There was no sign of anyone else, let alone a ten-thousand-strong army. He stifled a laugh.

That would cost several thousand weeks' allowance!

"That isn't going to be possible," he replied.

Kalunga clenched his bandaged fists in rage. He stood up to his full height. "You laugh at me, child?" he fumed. "And you deny my request? How dare you be so insolent!"

He stepped forward. Max shrank back in horror.

"I'm not laughing," protested Max. "And I don't have

access to thousands of flashlights. I could probably get you three."

Kalunga's disgusting, grimy teeth ground against each other. His eyes turned a deep shade of purple. Max scanned the chamber for a way out. But there only seemed to be one—the passage he came down. Idris and Sirus were standing right in front of it.

"I am growing impatient with my confinement here!" Kalunga snarled. "All I want to do is walk by the Nile during harvest time and see farmers turning shadufs in the fields."

Max swallowed nervously.

Shadufs in the fields? He remembered learning something about shadufs in school. They were some kind of farm tool used in ancient Egypt.

Kalunga glared at Max. "Oh, I may not have my full powers yet," the sorcerer hissed. "But when they are restored, I WILL

DEFEAT THE EVIL TULAMEN'S HEIRS! And I will gather with my fellow members of the Sorcerer's Circle!"

The Sorcerer's Circle? Hang on a minute. Is Kalunga thinking what I think he's thinking? Does he think we're still in ancient Egyptian times?

"Er . . . Kalunga, can you tell me what year it is?"

"DO NOT TRY AND BE CLEVER WITH ME!" screeched Kalunga. "I am the Pharaoh's Sorcerer. I know how to make the potion! We have come back to life fifty years after the death of Gazellion."

He's made some sort of potion to bring them back to life in fifty years...except he's got it very badly wrong.

"I hate to break this to you," Max said, "but it isn't fifty years after Gazellion's death."

Idris and Sirus looked confused.

Kalunga shook with rage. "DO NOT

INSULT ME!" he yelled. "I will turn you into a cockroach!"

In panic, Max quickly took off his digital watch. He held it up for Kalunga to see. "Do you think they had these fifty years after Gazellion's death?" He pressed the stopwatch function and then got the watch's alarm to beep.

"And what about the flashlight . . . I mean orb. That was invented way after your time. You must see that!"

Kalunga gaped at all of this in stunned silence. He shook his head several times. It was a while before he spoke again. "If what you say is true, then tell me, in which time are we actually living?"

Max took a deep breath. "It's about three

thousand years after Gazellion's death."

"*Three thousand years?*" Kalunga whispered in disbelief.

Max nodded.

Idris and Sirus gazed at each other with expressions of horror.

Kalunga's eyes narrowed in rage. "You lie!" he shrieked. He snapped his fingers. Idris and Sirus immediately stood to attention. Kalunga advanced towards Max. "Your life as a cockroach is about to begin!" screamed the mummy. "You are no match for the three of us!"

"WAIT!" cried Max in panic. He imagined himself scuttling over the sand with a hard shell on his back. "I can help you!"

"HELP ME?" raged Kalunga, nearly upon Max.

"Of course!" cried Max. "You've woken up way after the end of your civilization. You know nothing about the modern world! How

are you going to achieve anything? I can bring you items from this new world that will help. Help you with . . . whatever you're planning."

Kalunga suddenly stopped.

"That idea might have merit," he said, stroking his chin. "If what you say is true, we will need items from your time. When could you bring these?"

"Whenever you want," replied Max. He felt a tiny bit less terrified. "I'm staying up at the palace."

"The palace?" said Kalunga. His eyes widened in surprise.

Max nodded. "The Palace of Golden Kings."

Kalunga gave a grotesque smile. His teeth seemed to dance in his mouth. "The Palace of Golden Kings?" He placed a bandaged arm around Max's shoulder. "Why didn't you say so before? This is wonderful news!"

Max shivered as Kalunga squeezed his shoulder.

"Everything is different now," said Kalunga. "We can strike a deal!"

"We can?" asked Max. He flicked Kalunga's arm off his shoulder.

"Indeed," replied Kalunga. "I won't turn you into a cockroach if you bring me these present-day items. And do me a small favor concerning the palace."

"What favor?" asked Max suspiciously.

"I would like you to retrieve something of great personal value," Kalunga explained.

"A family heirloom. You see that Idris and Sirus have scarab beetle amulets round their necks?"

Max nodded.

"When I awoke, I found that mine had been stolen. It is not worth much. But it is of great sentimental value. It was taken from me before I was buried. And I have a pretty good idea who took it."

"Who?" asked Max.

"Inside Gazellion's palace is a workshop," said Kalunga. "This workshop belonged to the pharaoh's chief embalmer, Quodi."

An embalmer. What a delightful job!

"Quodi was—how should I put this—a bit of a thief. He was well-known for putting his fingers into more than just dead people's nostrils."

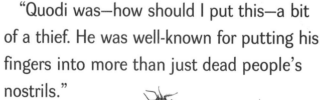

Gross!

"I believe that Quodi took my amulet before embalming me."

Max frowned. "There is one tiny problem," he said.

"Yes?" asked Kalunga.

"The palace isn't quite how it was when you left it. It's mostly buried under sand."

"I do not want excuses!" thundered Kalunga. The sweetness had gone from his voice. "Bring it back by nightfall with the modern items. Or you will find yourself turned into a disgusting cockroach!"

"If I bring you your amulet, perhaps you could do me a favor in return. Could you let me know what you've done with the *Sorcerer's Venom*?" asked Max.

"I wish to hear no more words from you!" thundered Kalunga. "BEGONE!"

Max decided not to chance his luck again. He headed for the doorway. But before he left, he turned around for a second. Sirus had just handed over his beetle amulet to Kalunga, who then vanished into thin air.

Where did he go? Could it be to the place where they've hidden the Sorcerer's Venom? I'll have to check it out when I return.

CHAPTER 13

The sun was really beating down now. Max walked back to the dig. As he walked on under the scorching sun, he thought about his conversation with Kalunga.

His snakes clearly snatched the Sorcerer's Venom. *He must have it somewhere in that pyramid! But where? And if he has it already, why isn't he using it? Is it because his powers are somehow "diminished"? What did the word "rejoin" refer to? And what's so special about this amulet?*

Max was exhausted by the time he arrived back at the site. But there was no time to rest. He knew Professor Blythe had warned him to stay away from the dig. But he had no choice. He found Cullen and another man inside a small orange tent. They were examining a wooden sword.

"Dad," called Max, "can I have a word?"

Cullen looked up. He said something to the other man and walked over to Max.

"How did it go?" Cullen asked.

Max gave him a quick, detailed report.

Cullen took it all in. He asked the same questions as Max about why Kalunga hadn't put the papyrus to evil use yet.

"Do you know anything about Quodi's workshop?" asked Max.

"As in Quodi the embalmer?"

Max nodded.

Cullen frowned. "The workshop's only just been dug out. Professor Blythe has ordered

that no one go in there yet. But we'll have to forget about that."

"Could you act as a decoy and get Blythe out of the way while I investigate?" asked Max. "I need to get my hands on that amulet. I think it might be more than just a trinket to Kalunga."

"Absolutely," replied Cullen.

Cullen quickly explained to Max where the embalmer's workshop was. Then he went off to find the professor.

Max checked that no one was looking. He rushed down the path Cullen had pointed out. On either side of the pathway were piles of rubble and pieces of stone. These jutted out from the ground at various angles. Some of them were fenced off.

A few minutes later, Max hurried down a small flight of stairs. He found himself in the hollow shell that had once been Quodi's workshop.

Max quickly pulled the Rock-Solid Scanner

out of his backpack.

OK, this can see two meters through any surface for up to five minutes. I'll have to work fast if I'm going to explore this whole room.

Max pressed the card flat against the wall to activate it. As soon as he did this, he could instantly see what was behind it.

He could make out the shape of some sort of cutting implement. But he saw no amulet. He moved the scanner up the wall. He swept the card across the left wall. And then onto the wall facing him. He saw various tools and knives. But nothing looked remotely like an amulet.

He checked his watch. He groaned with frustration. The five minutes were nearly up. There was no way he was going to be able to scan all of the walls in here.

But then an object came into view. Max breathed a sigh of relief.

There it was. No more then ten centimeters

behind the wall's surface
was Kalunga's red amulet.
It looked to be in perfect
condition.

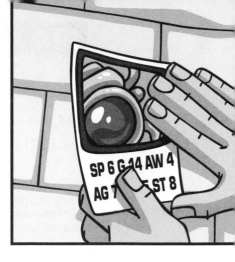

Max spun around. On
the floor beside him was a
trowel. He picked it up. He
began vigorously chipping away at the wall.
The stone started falling at Max's feet in small
chunks. There were other holes in the walls.
Surely an extra one wouldn't draw too much
attention?

Within five minutes, he could touch the
front of the amulet. But its sides were still
encrusted in stone.

*I need to be careful here. I don't want to
break it.*

He dropped the trowel. He picked up a small
chiseling tool with a tiny metal tip. Very gently,
he began to tap away at the stone. He worked
centimeter by centimeter. Soon, the amulet

was completely free. He pulled it out.

No sooner had he done that than the voice of Professor Blythe called out. "Who is down there?"

Max froze, amulet in hand.

Cullen must've let the professor get away. If he finds me here, it will be a complete DISASTER!

CHAPTER 14

Max thought about standing there and hiding the amulet behind his back. But his cheeks were flushed. He knew he would look guilty.

He scanned the workshop in desperation. The professor was coming down the steps.

"I said, who is that?" demanded Blythe.

Max's heart raced. If Blythe found him with the amulet, he'd have to hand it over. And that meant never finding out what Kalunga was up to. Not to mention that by the end of the day he'd be a cockroach!

He saw a low shelf at the other side of the workshop. A normal person would never be able to fit under this piece of stone. But Max Flash was no normal person. He ran over and threw himself facedown on the floor. He pressed himself down as hard as he could and squeezed under the shelf. He'd just pulled in his left arm when the professor entered.

Max forced himself as far back as possible.

"Hello?" called out Blythe.

Max listened to the professor's impatient breathing.

Blythe started walking around the workshop.

Suddenly his feet came into view. Max shrunk back. For a second, Max was convinced Blythe was going to crouch down and look straight into his hiding place.

"I could have sworn I heard someone in here," muttered the professor. A few moments later, Max heard him going back up the steps.

Max waited a couple of minutes before emerging. Then he hurried up the steps, clutching the amulet tightly.

At the top, Max checked left and right. There was no sign of the professor or of any other member of the dig team.

Max walked to the canteen. He strolled into the tent and up to the serving counter. He took a knife from one of the trays.

He slipped it into his pocket and hurried back to his tent.

Max crawled in and zipped the door flap closed behind him.

He pulled out the amulet and slid the knife under its lid. There was no give. He tried again, exerting more pressure. But still he couldn't get the lid to budge. Several beads of sweat snaked down his cheeks.

After a third unsuccessful try, he went outside and scoured the ground. A few meters away lay a small, sharp rock. He picked it up and took it back to the tent.

Now it was time for brute force.

I just have to be careful not to smash it. I don't think Kalunga would be happy about that.

Max turned the amulet on its side and brought the rock down hard. Nothing happened.

Maybe Kalunga put some kind of magic spell on it to stop it from being opened.

On Max's second attempt, the lid gave way. The amulet sprang open. Max took a deep breath and held it up.

Inside the amulet was a piece of papyrus that had been folded several times. Max's eyes widened.

What is this? It can't be the Sorcerer's Venom. *Kalunga got his snakes to grab that.*

Max carefully unfolded the papyrus. He saw that many of the hieroglyphs were exactly the same as the ones on the printout. And so were the pictures. There were the two-headed crocodile and the snakes around the border. Max stood there. He looked in confusion at this second piece of papyrus.

Is it a replica of the Sorcerer's Venom*?*

He stuffed it in his pocket and hurried off to find Cullen and Dodd. Ten minutes later, they were sitting at the table under the awning of their tent, studying the papyrus.

"But I don't get it," said Dodd. "Why are there two of them?"

"Let's think this through," said Cullen. "This Kalunga guy creates a potion to make him,

Idris, and Sirus come back to life fifty years after Gazellion's death."

"He said something about his ten-thousand-strong army and getting back at Tulamen's heirs," said Max. "Might his plan have been to come back to life after Tulamen was dead? And to reawaken Gazellion and snatch back the palace?"

Dodd looked impressed. "I reckon you're spot on," she said.

Max stared at the papyus. And that's when it hit him.

"That's it!" he whispered. "This papyrus isn't a copy of the *Sorcerer's Venom*. It's the other half. Kalunga must have torn it in two to stop it from falling into anyone else's hands. Quodi probably stole the amulet without realizing what was inside. That's what the mummies were talking about! Kalunga will get his full powers back when the two pieces are rejoined!"

Cullen and Dodd gazed at Max with open mouths. "That makes sense," said Cullen. "I bet his control of those snakes is limited because he doesn't have the whole papyrus. Perhaps his powers only work in and around the pyramid?"

"I have to take the amulet and some modern items back tonight," said Max.

"We can't risk letting Kalunga get his hands on this half of the *Sorcerer's Venom*," said Dodd. "When they're rejoined, anything could happen."

"I know," said Max. "I have to get both pieces before he does. But I have to deliver the amulet to him first. Come on, guys. I don't fancy being turned into a cockroach."

"Do you have any idea where the other piece of the *Sorcerer's Venom* might be?" asked Cullen.

"As I left, Kalunga seemed to vanish by a wall at the far side of the chamber. I want to find out where he went."

"That could be his magic," replied Dodd.

"It might be," nodded Max, "but it happened just after Sirus handed him his amulet."

"Definitely check it out," agreed Cullen. "But how will you buy yourself time? Kalunga is sure to open the amulet as soon as you hand it over."

"I'll trick him. I'll make him think he has both pieces. That will give me a chance to search the pyramid and find the other half. Let's seal up the amulet again. But put something in the papyrus's place," said Max.

"Hmmm," said Dodd. "But won't he open it right away?"

Cullen shook his head. "There's some amazingly powerful glue onsite," he said. "If we use that, it might take him a while to crack it."

"OK," said Dodd. "That's what we'll do. But if you're not back in two hours, we're coming to get you. Professor Blythe or no Professor

Blythe."

Max nodded, feeling his nerves fizzing up like millions of bubbles.

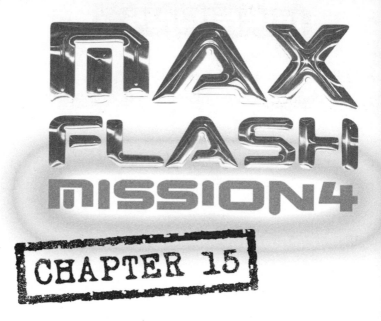

CHAPTER 15

As soon as the sky began to darken, Max made his move. Cullen and Dodd wished him lots of luck. They said they'd come looking for him if he wasn't back within two hours.

He headed to the pyramid. He went over his game plan in his head.

I give Kalunga the amulet. While he's trying to crack it open, I somehow locate the place where he vanished. I try to find the other half of the Sorcerer's Venom. *Then I get out of there. I race back to the site and accept Cullen*

*and Dodd's congratulations. Who knows? It
just might work!*

In his backpack, Max carried several
gadgets—exactly as Kalunga had asked. He
had his EX4 player, his M-CRASH 50 games
console, and a mini battery-operated kettle. It
was all that he could lay his hands on.

Max made good time to the pyramid. He
followed the passage down to the burial
chamber. Kalunga was waiting for him with
Idris and Sirus.

"So the orb boy returns," said Kalunga
darkly. "I believe you have several items for
me."

Max patted his backpack. "I have some
excellent pieces of twenty-first-century stuff in
here," he replied. "Shall I start with the EX4
player? It's super cool!"

"Let us put those aside for the moment,"
interrupted Kalunga. "I need to see if you have
completed your part of the bargain. Do you

have my amulet?"

He stuck out his hand.

Max reached inside his pocket and pulled out the amulet. "I've got it," he said. He showed it to Kalunga. "You'd better keep your promise of not turning me into a cockroach."

"Yes, yes," snapped Kalunga. He snatched the amulet from Max's hand. "I curse Quodi for thievery. And for delaying my plans. But now all is ready!"

He cradled it for a second as if it were a newborn baby. He tried to open the lid. It didn't budge. He frowned and tried again.

"I obviously secured it too tightly," he muttered.

Max saw his cue and took it. For years he took part in his parents' magic show. He had performed a variety of feats that involved taking things off people without them noticing. The trick was to direct their attention elsewhere and to perform the grab with the

utmost speed. All three of the mummies were concentrating on Kalunga's amulet. So that part was taken care of.

Max darted quietly behind the mummies. He snatched the amulet from around Sirus's neck. The mummy felt nothing. He continued to stare at Kalunga. Kulanga's frustration was rising by the minute.

"I WILL OPEN THIS!" he shouted.

Max quickly stole over to the wall where he had seen Kalunga disappear that morning.

It's only a hunch, but it's all I've got.

He studied the surface of the wall, looking for some kind of clue. But there was nothing.

"OPEN TO ME, O AMULET!" screeched Kalunga.

Max carried on scouring the wall. He spotted something. It was very faint, but it was definitely there—an image of a scarab beetle. It was exactly the same size as the beetles on the amulets.

Max glanced over his shoulder. The mummies were still struggling with the jammed lid.

Max held out the amulet and pressed it firmly against the beetle image on the wall.

If I'm right, there's something behind here. If I'm wrong...

For a few seconds nothing happened. Max could feel the sweat collecting on his forehead. He pressed the amulet harder. An

opening appeared in the wall. Max didn't
wait around. He jumped through the hole. He
heard a tiny whoosh as it sealed behind him.
He found himself in a wide tunnel. There was
a light about fifty meters ahead.

*Excellent! This must be where Kalunga
vanished. But where does it lead? And will the
other half of the papyrus be there?*

Max hurried down the tunnel. His heart was
racing.

*This could be the end of the mission.
I could be out of here soon with the whole
papyrus!*

He reached the end of the tunnel. He came
to a halt. He stared at the space that had
opened up before him. It was huge—at least
ten times the size of the servants' burial
chamber.

Wow! Now this is something else!
Wherever you looked, there was gold.
There were golden spears sunk into the

ground. There were huge gold vases. Shelves held gold plates and gold knives. And among all of this gold were jewels of every color and size. Giant red rubies sat next to turquoise diamonds.

In the exact center of the chamber, raised on a stone platform, was a solid gold

sarcophagus with ornate silver inscriptions on its side and a blue and silver lid.

This must be Gazellion's burial chamber! No wonder no one ever found it—it can only be accessed using those amulets!

But what grabbed Max's attention more than anything else were the astonishing

pictures on the chamber walls. There were huge numbers of Egyptian soldiers and weaponry. There were also strange beasts— like crocodiles with two heads and hippos with collars of razor-sharp blades. They were beautifully drawn. And they were exactly like the pictures on the two halves of the *Sorcerer's Venom.*

Max hoped that the amulet lid would hold tight. That would give him enough time to find the other piece of papyrus. He looked back to the tunnel entrance. There was no sign of movement. He couldn't hear a sound.

Great! Where shall I start looking? What about Gazellion's sarcophagus?

But as he hurried over to the giant casket, two arms reached out and grabbed him.

MAX FLASH MISSION 4

CHAPTER 16

What on earth . . . ?

Max twisted around. It was Kalunga and company. Idris and Sirus held him tight. Kalunga began wrapping him in mummy bandages.

"Thought we only had one entrance, fool?" snarled Kalunga.

Max thought of his Laser Stunner. He swung his arms out in an attempt to wrestle free. But he was no match for their combined strength.

The mummies bound him tighter still. Max's backpack fell to the floor. Moments later, he was completely tied up.

Kalunga shoved him to the ground beside the great, gold sarcophagus.

What is Kalunga going to do next?

"Did you really think you could get away with BETRAYING me?" screeched Kalunga. He held out his amulet. The lid was now open. Kalunga pulled out a rectangular piece of card. He shoved it in Max's face.

ONE DAY TRAVELCARD, it read.

"You stole what is mine!" seethed Kalunga. "And you replaced it with this worthless piece of junk!"

Max shook his head vigorously. "It's so not worthless," he protested. "It gives you unlimited travel on buses and trains between the hours of 9:30 A.M. and 5:00 P.M."

Kalunga looked at him with hatred.

"Think about it," Max went on. "You could

catch a movie, go shopping, or even visit a museum. Why not go to the British Museum? They have some of your mates in there."

"Stop this unspeakable drivel!" shrieked Kalunga. He ripped the travelcard in two and threw the pieces to the ground.

"WHERE IS IT?" he demanded. "Where is the other half of the *Sorcerer's Venom*?"

Do I lie and pretend I haven't got it? Or do I tell the truth? I think I'll go for the truth. Kalunga doesn't appear to have the other half. While he goes to get it, I will have small window of time to escape from these bandages.

"It's in my right trainer," Max announced.

"What's a trainer?" asked Sirus.

"It's a shoe," Max replied.

After some partial unwrapping of bandages, Kalunga finally retrieved the piece of papyrus.

"MAGNIFICENT!" yelled Kalunga, holding the papyrus high above his head.

"We are nearing the moment for the incantation of the *Sorcerer's Venom*!" he yelled with excitement.

An incantation? Isn't that some kind of chant?

Max's thoughts raced. *If it is a chant, I've got an idea. But I need my EX4 player.*

Max shuffled a few centimeters toward his backpack. He worked on loosening the bandages. He made sure the mummies weren't watching him.

The three of them were standing up. They were looking up at a plain clay vase that sat on a high wooden shelf. Kalunga waved his hand. The vase floated down toward him.

On the floor, Max was making good progress. He'd managed to work himself a little bit of space inside the bandages. He tugged and twisted his right arm. He could feel he was almost free!

Kalunga removed a piece of papyrus from the vase and unfolded it.

"I WILL NOW REJOIN THE TWO PARTS OF THE *SORCERER'S VENOM!*" he cried.

Come on! Just a few more twists and tugs!

Kalunga began bringing the halves of the papyrus together.

"REVENGE WILL BE OURS!" yelled Kalunga. Idris and Sirus stared at the papyrus. They were in awe.

Max pushed out his right arm.

I'm nearly there!

A split second later, the two pieces of papyrus came into contact with each other. Max watched in amazement as they fused together.

I have to break free!

The index finger of Max's right hand pushed through a gap in the bandages. Then he managed to push another finger through. He stretched out for his backpack. But he

couldn't quite reach it.

This is it! It's a do or die-a-cockroach moment!

MISSION4

CHAPTER 17

Max pushed his fingers out in one last effort.
To his relief, he managed to grab the top of
the backpack and inch it towards him.

"IT IS TIME FOR THE BATTLE. OUR ARMY
WILL RECAPTURE THE PALACE. GAZELLION
WILL BE PHARAOH ONCE MORE!"

Max stifled a laugh. He unzipped the
backpack and pulled out his EX4 player.

*An army? I'm sorry, but you three and
some twelve-year-old pharaoh kid don't make
an army. Even if you have the* Sorcerer's

Venom, *surely your four-person battle unit will be no match for the Egyptian army, air force, and navy!*

At that instant, Kalunga began his chant. It was performed in a screechy, high voice.

Max was ready for him. He pressed the RECORD button on his EX4 player. He began to loosen the remaining bandages. But he wanted to keep them around him so Kalunga would suspect nothing.

Kalunga's chanting continued. But to Max's surprise, nothing seemed to be happening.

Is this it? Is this my punishment? Will I be listening to this awful sound for eternity?

Then a strange swirling sound began to fill the chamber. To start with, it was very quiet. Almost too quiet to hear. But it was getting louder by the second. The border around the papyrus glowed a dark shade of red.

Kalunga's chanting was now almost deafening. There was a great vortex of swirling noise. And then Max noticed something. At first he thought his eyes were playing some sort of trick on him.

It was the pictures on the chamber walls.

The soldiers, spear-carriers, and wild beasts were all starting to shake and jiggle about.

What on earth...?

The figures on the wall were now rocking and twitching violently.

"YESSSSSSSSSSSSSSSSSSS!" shouted Kalunga.

And then suddenly, one of the pictures turned forward. A tall, bearded soldier carrying a sleek silver spear jumped off the wall. It was bizarre. A 2-D figure standing in a 3-D world.

Slowly, the soldier's 2-D features started swelling. First his head and then his arms. It looked like someone was using a bicycle pump to inflate him. Now his legs were puffing out and lastly his spear.

So this is the magic!

The transformation was now complete. A 2-D figure had become a 3-D figure. The figure on the wall became a real, armed soldier who was ready for battle.

"MAY THE EXIT OPEN!" shouted Kalunga above the unbelievable din.

At the far side of the chamber, a section of the stone wall slid open. This revealed a short, sandy path leading out of the pyramid.

The soldier shook his body as he adapted to being fully formed. A second soldier leaped out from the wall. This guy was stockier than the first. He carried a black dagger.

"MAY OUR ARMY PREPARE ITSELF!" yelled Kalunga.

At this cue, the two soldiers straightened themselves up. They marched through the opening and out into the desert.

A third and a fourth soldier popped out. They followed their comrades outside. More and more soldiers started flying off the walls. As soon as they hit the ground, they made straight for the exit.

Max's eyes bulged. There was a huge number of warriors.

So this is the ten-thousand-strong army!

And then the beasts started coming. The first was a lion. It had a ring through its nose and spikes covering its entire body.

A cozy family pet? I don't think so!

Next was a line of two-headed crocodiles. They had a look of bloodcurdling menace on

their double faces. Next came the hippos, with their spiky collars. Then a flock of large birds flew out. Their talons looked as sharp as daggers.

Kalunga carried on with his chant. His eyes lit up with joy at the miraculous act he was performing.

Ten minutes later, the last of the warriors and beasts had appeared and marched outside. There stood a massive and hideous army that would be able to take on any challenger!

MAX FLASH MISSION4

CHAPTER 18

A moment later, the sound in the chamber stopped. The room fell silent.

Kalunga turned his gaze to Max. He quickly pulled his hands back inside the bandages.

"You see," said Kalunga. "My powers are immense. But only the *Sorcerer's Venom* can perform this magnificent act of reawakening!"

"Impressive," replied Max. "Now could you make these bandages 2-D and let me out of here?"

The sorcerer ignored him. He turned to Idris and Sirus. "Now it is time for us to return to our living bodies."

Kalunga pointed the papyrus at Idris and Sirus. Their bandages started unravelling at incredible speed. Max watched as their shriveled flesh became like new again.

In a few seconds, Idris and Sirus resumed their human forms. They were both about twenty years old. Idris had a long, thin face and grey eyes. Sirus was plumper. He had a huge shock of black hair that sat untidily on his head. They were both dressed in white servants' clothes.

"JOIN THE OTHERS!" commanded Kalunga.

Idris and Sirus hurried up the sandy path.

"And now it is my turn," hissed Kalunga. He raised the papyrus above him.

His bandages started unfurling. His flesh began to fill out into a living person. He was about fifty years old. He had a flowing grey

beard, short grey hair, and small, flashing grey eyes. He was wearing a long silver gown decorated with strange, black symbols.

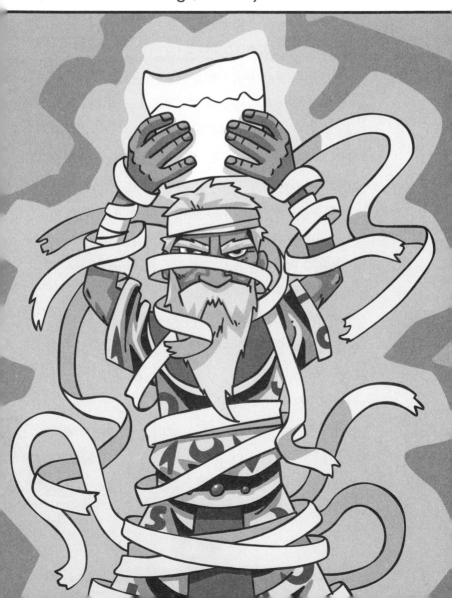

"Fancy letting me out of here now?" asked Max hopefully.

"Forget it!" snapped Kalunga.

He turned to the gold sarcophagus and pointed the papyrus at it.

"Master," Kalunga whispered, "we are ready for your return." The sarcophagus lid started to rise. When it was several meters in the air, it turned on its side. It hovered down to the floor.

Max stared at the sarcophagus. He was transfixed. He felt a mix of fear and excitement as a figure began to rise from inside the casket. Very slowly, the head and chest of the figure emerged. It was the body of a boy.

It's Gazellion! Right here, right now! If only I had a camera . . .

The boy pharaoh was

wearing a beautiful blue-and-gold ceremonial mask. It looked just like the one Max had seen in a TV show about Tutankhamen.

Kalunga bowed low. "I will go and prepare your army, Your Highness. When you have risen, come outside to inspect your troops. Then, if all is as you wish, we will set off immediately!"

Gazellion gave him a regal nod.

Kalunga looked down at Max. "As soon as our pharaoh has inspected his army, I will come back to deal with YOU!" he sneered. "I will make your life as a cockroach as unpleasant as possible!"

Max swallowed in fear.

Then Kalunga strode out of the chamber to join the troops.

CHAPTER 19

Max looked up at Gazellion. He was still sitting in his sarcophagus.

In one swift move, he threw off his bandages. Then he got to his feet.

"Isn't that mask a bit hot for you?" asked Max.

The pharaoh nodded. He raised his hands. He slowly lifted off the mask.

Sitting there was a boy who looked the same age as Max. He had smooth, tanned skin and deep-brown eyes.

"Gaz . . . I mean, Your Highness," said Max. "I have been charged with welcoming you back to the world. How are you feeling?"

"Tired, but content," replied the pharaoh. He smiled.

"It will be necessary for you to stay here for a short time," said Max. He had one eye on the path leading outside.

"What am I required to do during this period of waiting?" asked Gazellion.

Max suddenly remembered the rest of the contents of his backpack. He knelt down on the ground. He rummaged around for a couple of seconds. Then he whipped out his M-CRASH 50 games console. He flicked it on.

"You are required to play Lunar Chase 2233," Max replied with a bow. "I will explain to you how it works."

Gazellion looked confused. But Max showed him the controls. He passed the console to the pharaoh.

"What an excellent leisure-time pursuit!" grinned Gazellion once he'd got the hang of the game. "I can see many happy hours on the palace lawns with this wondrous item."

Max gave him a thumbs-up. He grabbed the ceremonial mask and his EX4 player and made for the exit. "I will be back shortly, Your Highness," he said.

But Gazellion was totally engrossed in the game and didn't look up.

CHAPTER 20

Outside the Denubi Pyramid stood a massive
ancient Egyptian army. They awaited the boy
Pharaoh. The men and beasts stood in long
rows. The night breeze kicked up some sand.
but the soldiers remained perfectly still. In front
of them, Kalunga stood tall and magnificent.
Idris and Sirus were at his side. He was still
holding the rejoined papyrus in his hand.

All heads turned. The boy pharaoh slowly
stepped out from the pyramid into the night
air. His ceremonial mask glittered as he strode

majestically to greet his mighty army.

Kalunga indicated a large rock on the ground. The pharaoh climbed

onto the platform and surveyed his troops.

The face of every soldier and beast held a look of dedication and determination. The battle was about to begin. They were ready for anything! The pharaoh stood there for a few seconds without moving. He looked down at the warriors.

Kalunga looked up. He frowned as he noticed a small object in the boy pharoah's hand. He didn't remember such an object being buried with his master.

The Pharaoh held the object out towards his troops. In one swift movement, he pressed down on something.

No sooner had he done that than a weird high-pitched sound started pouring out of the black-and-silver box.

Kalunga clenched his fists with rage. But it was too late . . .

The "pharaoh" ripped off the ceremonial mask. Underneath was the face of Max Flash.

When Max had heard Kalunga utter the word "incantation," he had decided what he must do. If Kalunga was going to use a chant to activate the full power of the papyrus, then the only way to reverse this would be to repeat the incantation backwards! And that's where Max's EX4 player had come in so handy. He'd recorded the whole chant. Now he was playing it backward to the troops. That was his way of undoing Kalunga's magic.

As soon as Kalunga realized what was

happening, he let out a furious cry. "STOP HIM!"

But at that instant, the reversed chant started to take effect.

One second, this huge army was standing at attention, awaiting the battle command. The next, the soldiers, creatures, and their weapons started to shake violently. There were cries of surprise, confusion, and fear.

In a more few seconds, they were all moving about wildly. They were like a speeded-up cartoon.

It's working!

Suddenly, their bodies began to deflate. For some, it was their feet that went first. For others, it was their heads. Wherever you looked, soldiers and beasts were popping back into 2-D form.

CHAPTER 21

"NOOOO!" screeched Kalunga. "WE WILL WIN THIS BATTLE!" But even as these words were coming out of his mouth, his face and body were becoming 2-D.

"HELP US!" pleaded Idris as his hands flattened out. These were followed by his arms and his torso. Sirus followed close behind.

Suddenly the whole 2-D army was sucked back into the pyramid. Max ran to watch as they hurtled through the opening. They were slapped back onto the chamber wall.

Max rushed over to Gazellion's sarcophagus. The boy pharaoh was sitting exactly where he'd left him. He was concentrating intensely on Max's handheld games console. He hadn't noticed any of the madness erupting around him. But before Max could reach him, Gazellion himself was flattened into 2-D. And so was Max's game!

No way! I saved for ages to get that!

As the pharaoh was pulled up on to the chamber wall, Max lunged towards Gazellion. But he was too late. Suddenly a hand grabbed his arm. He turned around and saw Kalunga. The sorcerer was all 2-D. Except for his right hand, which now held Max.

Max felt a popping sensation in his toes. He looked down in horror. He saw that they'd gone 2-D.

Not me as well!

His feet went next. And then his shins and knees. The 2-D effect was spreading through

his body. He was only centimeters from the wall. Max's thighs went 2-D as well. He felt his stomach flattening out. In a few seconds, he would be on the wall.

The 2-D effect was traveling down his arms. Soon they were completely flat. And his wrists were starting to go too. His body crunched against the wall. The 2-D parts of him stuck straight to it. And then he remembered the Laser Stunner.

Quickly!

Max aimed the bracelet at Kalunga. He pressed on it. Immediately, a white laser shot out, catching Kalunga full in the face. He screamed in agony and let go of Max.

Max pressed forward as hard as he could.

But his 2-D parts were resistant to being peeled off the walls.

Max tried again. He put all of his energy into one pushing movement. Suddenly, he felt his stomach leave the wall. This was followed by his arms, his legs, and finally his feet.

He fell to the floor and lay there for a few seconds. He breathed hard and tried to process what had just happened. He got up slowly. He was unsure if the battle was truly over. But the figures on the wall were now completely frozen. They had been reduced to pictures.

Max stood up. He walked closer to the wall. He was still on his guard just in case Kalunga had any other tricks up his 2-D sleeves. But there was the sorcerer. His face was frozen in a furious expression. His tiny beady eyes looked out from the wall in fury. Wherever Max stood, Kalunga's gaze seemed to follow.

And up there on the wall, in Kalunga's left hand, was the *Sorcerer's Venom*.

I think I can safely say it's going to be pretty useless to anyone now!

Max stretched his limbs. He checked to see that he had returned to his full 3-D form.

He was all there.

Then he walked up the pathway, through the opening, and began the trek back to the site.

I've got quite a story to tell Cullen and Dodd!

CHAPTER 22

The two DFEA agents were astounded by Max's adventure.

"If you hadn't sent that army back to their rightful place on that wall," said Cullen, "then all hell would have broken loose. We would have failed our mission. And let an ancient Egyptian army march on Cairo."

"Too right," agreed Dodd. "Can you imagine what would have happened? You'd have had a gigantic battle between modern and ancient, with all sorts of magic and sorcery thrown in."

Max suddenly caught sight of Professor Blythe. He'd completely forgotten about him!

Dodd seemed to read his mind. "You're thinking we should tell the professor, right?"

Max nodded.

"He needs to be shown Gazellion's chamber," said Cullen. "And I have an idea who should act as his guide."

Together they went over to the professor. He wasn't that happy to see Max. And he was even less happy about the idea of leaving his dig.

"But the Denubi Pyramid has been thoroughly excavated," he said irritably. "There's nothing new to discover there."

"I promise you it will be worth it," Cullen reassured him.

The professor complained the whole jeep ride to the pyramid.

But as the jeep drove around the perimeter and the large opening came into view, his mouth dropped open. The vehicle drew to a halt. They jumped out.

Max led him inside. The professor gazed around Gazellion's burial chamber in stunned silence. When he finally found his voice, he turned to face Max.

"And YOU discovered all of this?" he exclaimed, his face a mix of awe and delight.

Max nodded.

"But it's odd that Gazellion isn't inside his sarcophagus," muttered the professor.

"We do have his ceremonial mask," said Max. He pointed out the blue-and-gold mask.

"What a fine idea it was to have you on my dig. I've always thought children have a big part to play in matters of excavation," said the professor.

"Many more people will believe it's all genuine if you say YOU found it," said Max.

"Now that would be totally unfair and unacceptable," the professor replied with a stern shake of his head.

"Think of what other archaeologists would say," Max insisted.

The professor's resolute expression quickly melted. "There is that." He nodded with a faraway look in his eyes. "Maybe it would be a good idea . . . All in the interests of archaeology, of course."

"Of course!" agreed Max.

But the professor had noticed something else. He was striding across the chamber toward the wall on which the image of Gazellion had been imprinted.

Blythe took out a magnifying glass and held it up to the image of the boy pharaoh. Max exchanged looks with Cullen and Dodd.

"Remarkable," observed the professor. He called Max over. "You see that thing the pharaoh figure is holding?"

Max followed his gaze and winced.

"I know this sounds strange," went on Blythe. "But that looks remarkably similar to one of those handheld game thingies."

"Weird, isn't it," agreed Max sheepishly. "But I suppose lots of ancient things look quite like modern things, don't they?"

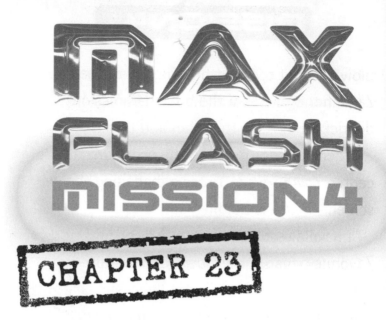

CHAPTER 23

Three hours later, Max, Cullen, and Dodd
were on a flight home. Max's dad was waiting
at the airport. He gave Max a big hug. He
shook hands with Cullen and Dodd.

"Your son did us proud out there," said
Cullen.

"Yes," agreed Dodd. "Without him, chaos
would have ensued."

Max went over all the details of his mission
with his dad on the drive home. When they
got back, Mom said she wanted a blow-by-

blow account too. But first he had to see Zavonne, who was waiting for the mission debrief.

When Max got down to the communications center, Zavonne's face was already on the screen.

"I have already spoken to Cullen and Dodd," Zavonne began. "They were full of praise for you."

At last! Zavonne is finally going to say something positive about me!

"However, I think you should have replaced Gazellion's sarcophagus lid before showing the chamber to Professor Blythe," she said.

Max was dumbfounded.

"But it weighed a ton," he protested.

"There are ways and means," Zavonne replied.

Max tried not to feel disappointed. But he couldn't help it. Would the DFEA ice queen ever praise him?

"And you're sure the *Sorcerer's Venom* is safely on the chamber wall?" she asked.

"One hundred percent," Max replied. "I don't think it'll be troubling anyone again."

"That is satisfactory," replied Zavonne.

"Er, Zavonne," said Max. "There is something I wanted to ask you."

"Go on," she said.

"In the battle to turn all of the 3-D figures back to 2-D, Gazellion took my handheld game console with him. It's up there on the wall, too."

Zavonne arched an eyebrow. "What are you getting at?" she asked.

Max swallowed nervously. "I'm asking whether the DFEA could buy me a replacement under their wear-and-tear guidelines."

Zavonne tutted. "We have no such guidelines," she replied. "If an article gets damaged, the operative is expected to replace it."

Wow! She's big on perks, isn't she?

"How about paying for half—"

But Max didn't get to finish. The image of Zavonne disappeared from the screen.

The cheek of it, thought Max. He wandered upstairs to find his parents and to get something decent to eat. *I put myself in grave danger and lose the console for my troubles! That doesn't seem fair!*

EPILOGUE

"Psst," whispered Sirus.

"What is it?" asked Idris.

"Do you reckon there are any 2-D bakers around here who might make 2-D bread?"

Idris sighed. "We're only drawings now, Sirus. We don't need to eat."

"But I'm hungry," Sirus moaned. "And my tummy is complaining."

"Why don't you have a go on that games console Gazellion was using? It'll take your mind off things."

Sirus thought about this.

"Your Highness!" called Idris. "Can Sirus borrow that games thingy?"

"I haven't got it," replied Gazellion.

"I'VE got it," hissed Kalunga. "And I'm nearly on level 5 of *Goblin Supremacy*. No one gets it until I'm on level 10."

Sirus sighed wearily.

"How about counting grains of sand on the floor out there in the burial chamber?" suggested Idris.

"We already did that," said Sirus.

"Well, let's try again," said Idris.

Sirus felt his tummy rumble. "OK," he conceded. "I'll start. 1, 2, 3 . . . "

MAX FLASH
MISSION 5
SUBZERO

Jonny Zucker
Illustrated by Ned Woodman